Onyx Kids

Shiloh's School Dayz

Book Four

The Secret Santa

By Rita Onyx

Onyx Star Publishing, LLC
Delaware, USA

Published by Onyx Star Publishing, LLC
Delaware.
http://www.onyxstarpublishing.com/

For publishing and distribution inquiries contact:
contact@onyxstarpublishing.com

Printed in the United States of America

Cover art by Sinead Onyx
Illustrations by Shalom Onyx

Onyx Kids is a trademark of Onyx Star Media LLC

Table of Contents

Chapter 1

Cold Winter Morning

It was a cold Saturday morning. Shiloh had the blankets pulled over his head. Shiloh's mom and dad tried to get him and his sister up early for school on the weekdays, but on weekends, they slept in. They slept all the way in. For as long as possible. So long sometimes that their parents would wonder if they were trying to break a world record.

Shiloh was frequently a few minutes late for school and his homeroom teacher

Ms. Sufferin was always watching him closely. Lots of students were a few minutes late, but Shiloh felt that Ms. Sufferin, was always picking on him. Anytime he was even just one minute late, she would slap her pointer down on his desk and talk about him in front of the class. Then she would start yelling at the class if they started to talk or laugh at what she said.

"Shiloh," she would start sickeningly sweet with his name, "Your lack of punctuality shows your disinterest in your studies, unless you have neglected to inform me that something is wrong with your legs. Do you have mobility issues?"

Shiloh would mumble, "I'm sorry, Ms. Sufferin. There's nothing wrong with my legs."

"Is something wrong with your alarm clock? Did you accidentally program it for pm instead of am?" She continued her questions.

"No," Shiloh would respond.

"Did you somehow trick your parents into thinking that school starts later?" Ms. Sufferin had her hands folded and her eyebrows raised as if that was really a serious question.

The class would start snickering.

"Quiet!" She snapped her head up to scowl at the rest of the class.

"No, my parents know what time school starts," Shiloh said.

"I thought so," Ms. Sufferin would say. "I'm afraid then that your brain is the culprit. Perhaps in the morning you prefer to remain in dreamland. Is that it?"

"Well…" Shiloh would try and respond in a way that was not snarky or disrespectful but would usually just stay quiet.

By this time, she would have to drop her criticisms so that she could start homeroom.

On the weekends, Shiloh's parents usually got up at the regular time. They often wandered down to the kitchen in their pajamas to have a cup of tea or hot chocolate and have quiet time to talk and scroll on their phones. Shiloh knew they enjoyed having some time alone without him and his older sister Shasha around to start asking questions and take over their conversations.

Shiloh opened one eye and peeked out from under the covers to look at his alarm clock. He had slept an hour later than he thought he had. It was almost 10 o'clock. He rolled over in bed and pulled the covers around his shoulders. As soon as he did that his feet stuck out from the blanket and he felt something warm, wet, and slobbery on his toes. It was Shadow his dog trying to get him to wake up.

"Stop that, Shadow, it tickles," said Shiloh. When Shadow continued, Shiloh used his feet to gently push him off the bed. Shadow whined a little and then went off into a corner of Shiloh's bedroom to sulk.

As he repositioned his arms, Shiloh heard a text coming in on his phone. *I wonder who that is,* he thought to himself. He grabbed the phone off his nightstand and fell halfway out of bed for a second. Then, he sat up.

It was a text from his best friend Evan:

> ```
> Are you doing
> anything special
> today?
> Can you meet me and
> Desirae at the
> secret lab?
> ```

He texted back:

> ```
> Secret lab on a
> Saturday? How'd you
> get in?
> ```

Evan wrote back within seconds:

> ```
> Sports activities
> going on. Some
> doors were open.
> I have my ways even
> without that.
> ```

Shiloh thought about it for a minute. He had planned to spend a lazy day at home. Despite the cold weather, he was going to take Shadow out for a walk and his dad had asked him to help him shovel snow around the house. But now, Evan had him curious. He wondered what Evan was doing. His friend was always coming up with crazy new inventions that he would store in the secret lab that only he, Evan, and Desirae knew about.

The secret lab was down in Cornerstone Middle School's deep, dark basement. None of the teachers had realized that Evan was using it as his own private lab. There was an old printing press and lots of ancient electronic equipment down there. There were flasks and remnants of a science lab from decades before too. Evan didn't waste anything. He used every piece of wire and every circuit he found. He usually had more than one invention going on at the same time. Shiloh often wondered how he kept it all straight. It was kind of creepy in the lab, but Evan's energy made it seem like something important might happen there at any moment.

Shiloh wrote back:

> I'll try to be there. My dad asked me yesterday to help him shovel snow. Let me see if I can get out of it.

Shiloh walked downstairs with Shadow at his heels. His parents hadn't heard him come down and he caught them cuddling on the window seat together under a blanket. They both had cups of hot chocolate in their hands. Shiloh stopped for a moment and peered in at them through the kitchen doorway. For a second, Shiloh tried to imagine how his parents would have looked before his older sister Shasha was born. Of course, there were pictures around their house but Shiloh tried to visualize them young and without children. It was such a strange feeling because he couldn't imagine them as young as him or even as a young married couple. To Shiloh, they were always the age they were now, kinda old.

Shadow was jumping up and down behind him as Shiloh cleared his throat so his parents would know he was there and then he headed into the kitchen.

"Hey, what brings you down here at this early hour?" his dad joked as Shadow ran over to him at the window seat to get the back of his neck scratched.

"Is it okay with you guys if I go over to Cornerstone today?" Shiloh asked.

"You want to go to school on a Saturday?" his mom asked. One of her eyebrows was raised higher than the other out of suspicion.

"Evan asked me to come by. He's got some project going on," said Shiloh.

"Is it something for science class?" asked his dad.

"Probably," said Shiloh, "but he didn't tell me yet. You know Evan. He loves to be mysterious."

"Well, we don't want to get in the way of the progress of science," said his mom as she smiled at Shiloh's dad.

"Does that mean I can go?" Shiloh asked.

"Yep!" said his dad. "Have a good time. I'll catch you next time for snow patrol. Guess I'll be getting my exercise today."

"I might be persuaded to come help you. I haven't shoveled any snow for a while," said Shiloh's mom. When both Shiloh and his dad just stared at her and remained quiet, she quipped, "Hey! I'm stronger than I look." She flexed her arms to try and prove her point.

"Sounds like a plan," said Shiloh's dad, still looking unconvinced.

As Shiloh's mom playfully swatted her husband, Shasha came bounding down the downstairs. She was wearing red and white striped pajamas and her hair looked like it had been electrified. "Good morning everybody."

"Did we wake you up, honey?" asked their mom.

"No, I've been awake for a while. I was reading a book in bed," said Shasha. She turned to Shiloh. "I thought I heard you say you were going to school today. That can't be right." She nodded her head in disbelief.

"Actually I am. Evan wants help on his science project," said Shiloh.

"Evan's a genius. Why would he want your help?" Shasha wouldn't let up with her questions.

"Because he just needs my help," Shiloh tried to sound convincing to his parents while he fixed Shasha with a stare that said BE QUIET BEFORE I HAVE TO GO AND SHOVEL SNOW!

Thankfully Shasha got the hint and just shrugged and poured herself some juice.

"Do you guys remember the Gansley mansion that was for sale?" Mom asked.

"Didn't some rich techie couple buy it in August?" Shasha said. "Shiloh, they're rich because they used to live and work where they make a lot of apps and stuff. It's called Silicon Valley," said Shasha.

"Yes, that's right," said their mom. She got up from the window seat to pour more hot chocolate from the steaming stovetop pitcher into her mug.

"My best friend Shayna told me that she met those people," said Shasha.

"Really?" their mom said. She had spilled a couple of drops of hot chocolate on the countertop and was wiping it off.

"Yeah, her dad works with them," said Shasha.

"When I talk to Shayna's mom, I'll mention that I know them," said their mom.

"Shayna said that they are doing all these cool things inside the house and they're almost done. She said their house was going to be in the Christmas open house tour," said Shasha.

"Is that the tour where you get to see the inside of all the mansions?" Shiloh asked.

"Yes," said his mom.

"That's cool," said Shiloh, "I can't wait to see what they've done with the inside of it. What if there's a trap door!"

"Why would they put that in their house?" Shasha asked. "Think Shiloh."

"I dunno, that's what I would do if I could," Shiloh said. "And I'd make sure you went in it," he muttered softly.

15

"What did you say?" Shasha asked.

"Well, this pajama party has been fun," said their dad, who gave Shiloh a look that told him that he heard what he said. "but I think we should all get showered and ready for some breakfast. Anybody up for some whole grain pancakes?"

"Yum!" said Shasha. "I could go for those."

Shiloh made a face. "Wish I could stay, but now that you guys said I could go I better head out," said Shiloh. "In fact, I better go text Evan now."

"Okay, just check in with us before you leave," said Shiloh's mom.

Shiloh ran upstairs, grabbed his phone, and texted Evan.

> Mom and Dad said
> okay, but I still
> have to shower
> and head out. I'll
> have to ride my
> bike over

```
so it will take a
while.
```

Evan texted back in a few seconds.

```
Great! Hurry up
though!
```

After Shiloh showered and put on some joggers, he raced downstairs. His mom was in the kitchen, but his dad and Shasha hadn't come down yet.

"Do you want to take anything to eat?" his mom asked.

"Maybe a couple of granola bars," said Shiloh.

"You'll have to let me know about Evan's project when you come home," said his mom. She had dressed in some jeans and an old shirt so she could help Shiloh's dad with the snow shoveling later on. It made Shiloh feel a little guilty that she was going to be stuck with his chore.

"Sorry, you're stuck with the shoveling, Mom," said Shiloh.

17

"That's okay. I don't mind. Maybe I can throw a snowball or two at your dad. It'll be fun," she said as she smiled and handed him the granola bars and a chocolate bar too. She had a secret stash in the kitchen that Shiloh's dad didn't know about. Shiloh's dad was a health nut and discouraged her from buying sugary things. That's why Shiloh had been so surprised when he had seen them drinking hot chocolate.

Shiloh had just stuck everything in his backpack when his dad walked downstairs.
"Do you want a lift to Cornerstone?" his dad asked. "I can take you."

"No, that's okay. I need a way to get back so I'll ride my bike," said Shiloh.

"It's a pretty long ride. Are you sure?" asked his dad.

"Yup! Sorry that I'm missing your famous whole-grain pancakes," said Shiloh.

"No worries. I just hope your mom didn't give you too many sugary snacks to take with you," his dad said as he knowingly glanced first at Shiloh and then at Shiloh's mom.

But, Shiloh and his mom didn't show their secret in their faces.

Chapter 2

Secret Santa's Secret Lab

By the time Shiloh had ridden his bike to Cornerstone, he was tired out. He had forgotten how cold the winter wind would feel around his face. There were lots of kids outside getting ready to participate in sports activities. Shiloh hadn't joined a sport team this year because he was too busy. There was always so much to do with his schoolwork and family activities that he decided to take a break.

When he got inside one of the school's open doors, he looked around carefully to make sure that none of the teachers were around. Evan had managed to keep his lab secret so far and Shiloh didn't want them to be busted. At the end of the hallway, there was a door that was marked *Staff Only,* but it was clear that it wasn't being actively used because the "S" and the top of the "t" were partly wiped out. The missing parts of the letters made it look like it was labeled "laff Only." It made Shiloh smile every time he looked at it. After Shiloh pushed open the heavy door, there was a winding metal staircase that led to the basement. It was a dark, scary-looking place and Shiloh often wondered if that was the reason that the teachers and the principal had forgotten all about it.

Shiloh was just about to swing open the door to the secret lab when he paused for a second. He could hear some quiet Christmas music playing, but he wasn't prepared for what he saw when he swung open the door. The lab, which was usually a chaotic mess of old electronic parts and science equipment, had been transformed into a winter wonderland. It reminded Shiloh of one of those houses with the huge amount of Christmas lights except it was indoors. It didn't even smell like vinegar, instead there was a subtle smell of pine and cinnamon.

"Wow! How did this happen?" asked Shiloh. He was trying to take everything in, but it wasn't easy.

Evan smiled, "Glad you could make it. Desirae and I couldn't wait to see the look on your face when you saw it."

"We've been working on it for a couple weeks," said Desirae. "Evan and I have been coming down here every chance we could get."

Along one side of the room was a long, wooden ramp that Evan had built. "What's this?" asked Shiloh.

"Take one of the steel balls in the box and start it at the top of the ramp," Evan said.

Shiloh lifted one of the steel balls up and then placed it carefully at the high point of the ramp. Then, he let it go. The ball started to roll down and as it did it hit bells at the side. By the time it got to the bottom it had played a section of *Jingle Bells.*

"That is unbelievably cool, Evan. How did you figure it out?" Shiloh asked. He was ready to try the ramp again and push the ball so it would play a little faster.

"I've been working on that project since October off and on. I built a scale model in my bedroom as a prototype," said Evan. "It's based on the ramp Galileo built to test his theories about gravity and acceleration." Evan was such a science geek, but in a cool way. He made their lives very interesting.

Shiloh let another ball loose and pushed it with his hand. The ball rang the bells faster and hit the perfect tones for *Jingle Bells.*

Then, Shiloh walked over to the opposite wall. There, Evan and Desirae had set up Evan's model train with a Christmas village. Before Shiloh could say anything, Evan spoke up, "I haven't had the room to set up this train at home. I wanted to set it up in our garage, but you know how my parents are about their retro car. They can't have that car in the driveway subjected to the wind and snow. I even thought about fixing up our attic and setting it up there, but it's just too hot. Even in the winter, when the heat is on inside the house, it gets too hot up there. But this is the perfect spot for it. Desirae and I found an old ping-pong table and carted it here last week."

"How did you get the table down the spiral staircase?" Shiloh asked.

"It wasn't easy," said Desirae as she laughed. "Evan set up this gizmo that helped us lower it down. It was almost too much for us."

"Why didn't you ask for my help?" asked Shiloh.

"It was kind of a two-person job," said Evan. He cleared his throat and pointedly nodded at Desirae while she was turned around.

Shiloh understood now. Evan wanted some one-on-one time alone with Desirae. He knew that Evan had had a crush on Desirae ever since she had won the school science competition with her hand-held earthquake detector. It didn't hurt that Desirae was so smart, but the fact that she was pretty and sweet sealed the deal for Evan. Shiloh liked Desirae a lot too but not the same way Evan did. He had been thinking about their other friend Roxy more and more. Maybe he could invite her down here to see this amazing site since she already knew about the secret lab.

"Let's call Roxy and ask her to come and see all of this. She'd love it!" Shiloh exclaimed.

Desirae's smile immediately disappeared. While Evan really liked her, she had eyes for Shiloh. It was complicated.

"Why don't we call her tomorrow. We have a lot more to show you and a huge surprise at the end," said Desirae.

"Oh ok. Can I turn the train on to see how it works?" asked Shiloh.

"We thought you'd never ask," said Desirae. She was excited to see Shiloh's reaction.

The modern, streamlined train took off on the surface of the ping-pong table, which had been transformed to look like a railway station. Once it took off from the station it went by the Christmas village. The village had a downtown section with shops that were lit up with colorful lights. In the center of the village was a tiny pine tree that almost looked real. It was decorated with miniature ornaments and lights. As the train went past, the lights in the surrounding houses flipped on in succession. It gave the illusion that people in their houses were turning on their indoor lights to see the train go past.

"It's amazing," said Shiloh. "The train is so cool and so are the shops and the houses."

"Desirae's responsible for those. She made them at home at night and then brought them in so we could build it a piece at a time," said Evan.

But Shiloh wasn't prepared for what happened next. All of a sudden, the train went down a ramp under the table. Desirae pulled a cord and the skirting attached to the bottom of the ping-pong table opened like curtains in a theater. Underneath was a sculpted mountain. The train

27

went around and around into tunnels and out and past dense pine forests until it ended up by the side of a miniature farm with a red barn and barnyard animals.

For a second, Shiloh squatted down so that he could see better. Then, he plopped down on the floor with his legs in a V-shape so that he could watch the colorful train speeding down the mountainside. He could almost imagine himself as a miniature passenger riding inside the train.

When the train finally stopped, Shiloh looked up at Evan and Desirae with amazement. "I think I have the world's most talented friends," said Shiloh. "I've never seen anything like this! How did you make this mountain?"

"Desirae's idea again," said Evan. "We made it from paper-mâché, you know, the material they make piñatas from."

"That's only partly of it," said Desirae. "Evan developed a better paste material that makes it stronger." Evan blushes. He always did when Desirae was complimenting him.

Shiloh stood up and looked all around. There were blinking color lights hanging on the walls and from the ceiling.

"There's more," said Evan, "but we, have to keep the sound down, there are too many people around today. We don't want to get found out."

Evan walked over to one of the many computers in the lab. He clicked open a software program. "Which carol would you like to hear?"

"I like *All I Want For Christmas Is You*," said Shiloh.

"I love that one too," said Desirae, dreamily, as she looked at Shiloh.

Evan cleared his throat to break Desirae out of her daydream. "Hmmmm...I don't know if I have that one programmed in," said Evan. "Wait! Here it is!"

The music started playing from the computer system and the lights turned on and off giving the illusion of an outdoor light show inside the secret lab.

After they listened to the whole song, Evan switched the lights to just stay on with intermittent flashing.

The three friends were quiet for a few seconds as Shiloh continued to look around. "That was fantastic! This isn't just your secret lab anymore, Evan. It's Santa's Secret Lab," said Shiloh.

"Exactly!" exclaimed Desirae. "That's part of what we want to talk to you about. This is the surprise!"

"We want to play Secret Santa to a lot of kids this year," said Evan. He walked over to a stand-up folding wall that was decorated with wooden cutouts of Santa and his reindeer team. "Just step behind this wall."

Shiloh walked behind the wall to see three tables set up in a row. Each table had a nameplate. Shiloh's nameplate was on the right, Evan's was on the left, and Desiree's was in the middle. There were old toys from flea markets set up on every table. There were also some new toys that looked like they might be Evan's inventions.

"What's all this?" asked Shiloh.

"It's our toy shop," said Evan. "You know the story behind Secret Santa, don't you?"

"No," said Shiloh. "We do a Secret Santa gift swap at my house every year, but because there are only four of us we can always match the gift to the giver. It's fun because we give each other corny gifts, but I don't know the history behind it."

"Well," said Evan. "There was a man by the name of Larry Dean Stewart. For two years in a row he lost his job right before Christmas. He was very depressed. He was having a cup of coffee at a drive-in and feeling very sorry for himself until he noticed a waitress. She was shivering in the cold as she delivered food and coffee to people's cars. He gave her $20 as a Christmas gift so she could buy a warm jacket and she got teary-eyed. A stranger had never given her a gift before. Eventually, Larry became wealthy as he built up a huge business in phone and cable services. He started giving $100 bills to needy people in his hometown of Kansas City. No one knew who he was. His identity was a secret until a few months before he passed away. He gave away over one million dollars over his lifetime and he trained other people to be Secret Santas too."

"Wow! What a story!" exclaimed Shiloh, "I wish I had $100 bills that I could hand out."

"That's why we're doing toys instead," said Desirae.

"We're going to repair and paint these toys," said Evan. "Some of them are old toys from our own

...tics and some are from flea markets. I'm building some too. Once we finish with them they'll be as good as new. Then, we'll wrap them up and deliver them to toy drives all over the city in time for Christmas."

"Look!" said Desirae. "I even designed a special Secret Santa tag we can put on them. Will you help us, Shiloh?"

Shiloh looked at Desirae's Secret Santa tag. Santa was dressed in a red and green detective's outfit. He even had a pipe like Sherlock Holmes.

"Of course I'll help!" said Shiloh. "I have a bunch of old toys I can contribute too. Shasha might as well. I really think Roxy should join us. Let's call her today. I'm sure she's going to want to help."

"But..." Desirae started to say something but was interrupted by Evan.

"That's a great idea. We'll make her a name plate too. Just tell her not to tell anyone else about Santa's Secret Lab," said Evan.

"I won't," said Shiloh, "but it's really *Secret* Santa's Secret Lab."

Shiloh picked up a small wooden boat. "I used to have one of these when I was three or four years old. I used to put it in a big plastic tub and play with it for hours."

"We have some water-resistant paint around," said Evan. Evan pointed to the old bright-yellow printing cabinet that was marked FLAMMABLE in big letters. "I got rid of all the old inks that were in there and put in the cans of paint and other supplies we need to fix the toys. If you rummage around in there, I'm sure you can find what you need."

Shiloh dug around in the cabinet until he found just the right blue and red paints for the boat. Desirae was stitching a button on a fabric doll and Evan was building a toy robot.

Shiloh texted Roxy and asked her to meet at the school. She was surprised that they were there on the weekend but she was eager to see what was going on. When she arrived, she was just as amazed as Shiloh.

"This is so cool!" Roxy exclaimed.

Shiloh took her around and showed her all the things that Desiree and Evan had showed him. When the tour was over she wanted to join in on all of the fun. They made a workstation for her and she got to work fixing toys as they all jammed to some upbeat Christmas music.

Chapter 3

Family Christmas Traditions

Evan, Shiloh, Desirae, and Roxy
worked on fixing toys for two hours.
They listened to Christmas music
and talked about the holiday season.
There was just another week before
school break and they were all
looking forward to spending time
with their families.

"What do you guys do at your
houses for Christmas?" Desirae
asked.

Evan spoke up first, "Well, my mom
and dad usually go to a Christmas

tree lot and get the biggest real tree possible for Christmas. Once in a while I go along, but most of the time they go by themselves so they can surprise me and my little brother Will."

"I didn't know you had a little brother, Evan," said Desirae. She was surprised. "How old is he?"

"He's in kindergarten," said Evan. "He'll be starting first grade next year."

"That's cool," said Desirae. "I think it would be fun to have a younger brother or sister. My two brothers are both older than me. What about you, Shiloh? What do you do at your house for Christmas?"

"Well, I try to talk my parents into a real tree every year, but about three years ago, my parents brought home a bug-infested tree by accident," said Shiloh, "and ever since then my mom refuses to have a real tree in the house."

Desirae laughed. "I forgot that your mom has a bug phobia. What kind of bugs were they?"

"About a million baby spiders...I thought they were cute since they were so tiny, but my mom freaked out," said Shiloh. "It took a long time to get rid of those spiders. They crawled everywhere."

"That is so gross!" Roxy said, looking horrified.

Evan cleared his throat, "Technically spiders are not bugs. They are arachnids. Did you know that some people put spider ornaments on their trees and they believe that finding a spider on an indoor tree is good luck?"

"I stand corrected," said Desirae with some sarcasm in her voice, "but I already knew that spiders weren't bugs. Let's just say that Shiloh's mom has a creepy-crawly phobia. It is strange to think about spiders being thought of as good luck."

"I wonder where this came from," Roxy questioned.

"Well, it comes from an ancient folktale. I believe it's from the Ukraine," said Evan. "It's a story about a poor widow with two small children. A pinecone fell into a hole in their roof during a winter storm. The pine seeds fell out onto the dirt floor and a pine tree started to grow. The children were delighted because it meant they would have a small Christmas tree for the holiday but they didn't have any money to buy ornaments. There was a spider crawling around in the tree. The spider heard them and knew they were sad because they couldn't decorate their tree. So, on Christmas Eve she worked all night and decorated the tree with intertwined silky webs. On Christmas morning when they opened the shutters, light streamed in. There were delicate spider webs all over the tree, but they weren't just any spider webs. They were threads of silver and gold. That's why we decorate our trees with tinsel."

"I love that," said Desirae. "Maybe your mom wouldn't be so afraid of spiders if she heard that story, Shiloh."

The friends were quiet for a few minutes as they continued their work on the toys.
Evan had made it his goal to fix a bunch of broken wind-up toys before he went back home. He was working on a toy penguin that he had some success with. He wound up the back of the penguin toy and it managed to waddle all the way across the table before stopping. "I think Will would love this. I'm tempted to keep it out and give it to him for Christmas," said Evan.

"Why don't you? I don't see why you can't. We have a lot of other toys for our Secret Santa project," said Desirae.

"What do you do Desirae? You didn't tell us what you do over at your house for Christmas," said Roxy.

"I was hoping you would ask," Desirae said. "We have some unusual traditions. First of all, we have an artificial tree that looks almost real."

"That doesn't seem unusual," said Shiloh.

"I didn't tell you the unusual part yet. We hang our tree from the ceiling," said Desirae

"What? said Evan. "Why? Isn't there a huge gap between presents and the tree?"

"Because reasons. We did it before it became trendy a few years ago," said Desirae.

"This is a trend?" Asked Roxy.

"Yeah, Shasha tried to convince my mom to do that last year and she just laughed," said Shiloh. "Shasha always likes things she thinks are fashionable."

"It's a funny story," she said. "One year, before we started the hanging

41

tree tradition, my mom decided that she wanted to decorate the tree just with gingerbread ornaments. She did and it was absolutely beautiful. It was the nicest tree we ever had. Unfortunately, our two Labrador retrievers decided they were hungry early on Christmas morning. They knocked over the tree and started to eat the gingerbread cookies while we were still asleep upstairs."

"Oh no!" said Shiloh.

Evan's eyes went wide. "Did they get sick?"

"It wasn't too bad, but they were whining because their tummies hurt. My mother's beautiful tree was all over the floor and it took us a long time to get the gingerbread crumbs out of the carpet. It seems funny now, but it wasn't too funny then! I helped my mom clean all morning," said Desirae as she smiled.

"So, now you have a tree that no one can knock over," said Shiloh.

"Exactly!" said Desirae.

"What other traditions do you have?" Evan asked. He was wondering if he would ever be invited over to Desirae's house, her family sounded just as quirky as his was.

"Well, we don't decorate our tree until Christmas Eve and we have to stand on ladders to do it because it's closer to the ceiling than the floor," said Desirae.

"What's your favorite tradition?" asked Evan.

"Well, my favorite is the tradition we call *The Reading of the Christmas Books*," said Desirae. "There are five of us, so the ten days before Christmas we each pick two books that we want to read to everyone else."

"What kind of books?" Evan asked.

"Any kind of book we want as long as it's a Christmas story," said Desirae. "Some years, my dad reads *A Christmas Carol* by Dickens over two nights and he does the parts in different voices. It's so fun!"

"Hey guys, I just realized I never had any breakfast this morning. I'm starting to get hungry," said Shiloh.

"Me too," said Desirae.

"Same here," said Roxy.

Evan didn't hear either of them. He had been imagining what Christmas would be like with Desirae. He was so caught up with his wonderful future life with Desirae that it looked like he was in a trance.

"Earth to Evan. Earth to Evan," Shiloh said. "Is there any food around here?"

"Oh, sorry," said Evan. He had to snap out of his daydream right before he imagined Desirae about to kiss his cheek. "Didn't you have breakfast?"

"Nope. I rushed over. In fact, I turned down my dad's famous whole-grain pancakes just to be here," said Shiloh sarcastically.

"I'm sure that was hard." said Desirae, irritatingly, as she started to grab another torn-up rag doll that needed mending. "Maybe I can go to the cafeteria and see if there's anything I can grab for us."

"That'd be great," Shiloh said. "I'm afraid that if any of the teachers are there I'll get stopped."

"I agree," said Desirae. "If any of my teachers are around, I'm sure I can come up with some excuse so that they don't get suspicious. The last thing we want is for anyone to find Secret Santa's Secret Lab! I'll just finish stitching a button on for this doll's missing eye and then I'll go, but I could use some cash."

Roxy, Shiloh and Evan both stopped what they were doing and emptied out their pockets. Between the three of them they had about ten dollars. They handed the cash to Desirae.

"Thanks," said Desirae. "Any requests? Breakfast? Lunch?"

"I don't care at this point. As long as it's edible I'm good. Of course, if there's donuts with sprinkles I wouldn't complain," said Shiloh, but just as he said it he realized that he had the two granola bars and the chocolate bar that his mom had given him before he had left the house. He'd forgotten all about them. "Wait! I just remembered that I have some snacks stashed." He tore apart his backpack and took them out.

"Okay, but that's probably not enough. I'll go anyway," said Desirae. "And don't worry, Evan. I'll make sure that no one follows me on the way back. Is there anything you want, Evan?"

"Anything you like I like," said Evan as he smiled at Desirae.

Desirae blushed. Roxy snickered.

Shiloh rolled his eyes. "Dude that's too much," he whispered to Evan.

Desirae took her jacket with her. The jacket had deep pockets that were perfect to hoard snacks. She had decided to exit the school and then come back in so that no one would get an idea where she'd been. She walked out the lab door and tried to be quiet as she went up the winding metal staircase. No matter how softly she tiptoed, her steps on the metal staircase always seemed loud. Then, she pushed open the heavy door to the hallway. She turned around to make sure that it had shut behind her and smiled when she saw the "Staff Only" letters.

She found the closest exit door that wasn't locked and went outdoors. It had actually gotten colder than when she had arrived at Cornerstone in the morning even though it had stopped snowing. There were quite a few outdoor sports going on and some of the teachers were coaching. She pulled the hood up around her face so that she wouldn't be easy to recognize from a distance.

She walked all the way around to the front entrance. It was quiet and the entrance to the school seemed different than it did during the regular school week, but Desirae couldn't figure out exactly why. The front door even seemed heavier. The hallway was quiet with just a few students getting in and out of their lockers.

As she walked into the cafeteria, she smelled coffee, but she didn't see any of the teachers. There didn't seem to be any hot food in sight, but the vending machines had snacks so she walked up to them to see if she could find anything that Evan and Shiloh would like. She had almost decided on a package of miniature donuts and an apple turnover when she heard some noises behind her. It was Coach Robertson and Mr. Thomas. They were both dressed in sports gear and Mr. Thomas was carrying a box of donuts.

"Hi, Desirae!" said Mr. Thomas. "What are you doing here on a Saturday?"

"I like watching soccer practice," said Desirae as she smiled. She was hoping that Ms. Sufferin was not around since she and Mr. Thomas were often together.

"Coach Robertson asked me to help with the boys soccer team. I didn't see you out there. By the way, could you use some doughnuts?" Mr. Thomas asked.

"Sure," said Desirae, grateful he didn't ask any more questions. She tried not to act too excited for the free food. "A few of my friends are around too and will want some."

"Great, take them. They're just going to get stale by Monday if we put them in the fridge," said Coach Robertson. "We bought them for the players, but I guess we bought too many."

"Thanks!" said Desirae. She didn't open the box, but as she turned to walk away she saw Ms. Sufferin walking into the cafeteria.

Chapter 4

Secret Santa's Secret Elves

Uh, oh, Desirae thought to herself. *If she sees me it could be trouble.* Desirae quickly pulled up her hood and tried to bend her head so that Ms. Sufferin wouldn't notice her.

The temptation would have been to walk fast, but Desirae did the opposite. She walked casually so she wouldn't draw any attention to herself. The most difficult part about it was not laughing when she saw how Ms. Sufferin was dressed. She'd never seen Ms. Sufferin in any sportswear before. She looked like something out of the 80s and 1800s. Somehow, she managed to find an old fashioned dull, gray track suit and had a sweatband around her forehead. To make matters worse, she had on black boots. Who wears boots with jogging pants?

   As Desirae thought about what
Shiloh and Evan would have said
about the way she didn't realize that
Ms. Sufferin had seen her,

"You there!" Ms. Sufferin called.

Oh no! Desirae thought. She was
busted. Ms. Sufferin had the eyes of
an eagle and hearing like a dog.
Desirae tried to pretend she didn't
hear her and kept walking.

"Dez-uh-ray!!!" Ms. Sufferin called
her even louder and emphasized
each syllable.

Desirae stopped in her tracks and turned around. Ms. Sufferin was right behind her.

"What are you doing here? Why do you have so many donuts? Why are you walking towards the classroom? There closed," Ms. Sufferin asked all at once.

"Um..." Desirae paused, unsure of how to respond. She knew that Ms. Sufferin was sharp and would catch even a hint of a lie.

"Um is not a word. Well, technically it is, but I don't like it! You tell me now young lady, and you tell me the truth," Ms. Sufferin peered down at her from behind her enormous glasses.

Desirae was about to say something but luckily, Ms. Sufferin was distracted when she saw Mr. Thomas. She didn't even wait for an answer before she headed for him.

Desirae couldn't believe her luck. She was so thankful that Ms. Sufferin was sweet on Mr. Thomas.

When the cafeteria door swung behind her, Desirae breathed a sigh of relief. She carefully wound her way through the hallways until she came to the abandoned one that led to the secret lab. The "laff Only" door seemed heavier than usual as she pushed it to gain access to the winding metal staircase. She had been paying very careful attention to make sure that no one was following her.

Finally, she pushed open the door to the lab. Shiloh, Evan, and Roxy had been taking a break and were watching the electric train. Desirae felt so much better now that she had reached the lab safely without getting caught.

"What's this?" asked Shiloh as he got up from his squatting position. He had been watching the train go in and out of the mountain tunnels.

"Donuts!" exclaimed Evan. "How did you get such a big box?"

"I ran into Coach Robertson and Mr. Thomas in the cafeteria. They bought too many doughnuts for the players so they gave me these," said Desirae, "I couldn't believe it."

She set the box down on an empty table and then lifted the cover. Inside were a dozen of the most delicious looking donuts they had ever seen. There were glazed donuts with green and red sprinkles, there were chocolate-dipped donuts, both cake and glazed, and there were filled donuts shaped and decorated like Santa and his reindeer.

"My dad would have a fit if he saw all this sugar," said Shiloh.

"I'm getting a sugar buzz just looking at them," said Evan as he laughed.

"Guess who else I ran into," said Desirae. The way she said it made it quite obvious.

"Oh, no! Ms. Sufferin was with them?" asked Roxy.

"Did she notice you?" asked Evan.

"Yes, but I managed to sneak away when she saw Mr. Thomas. I had to try not to laugh when I saw her though. She was dressed like she was in a weird time warp," Desirae said.

"I gotta see that," said Shiloh as he laughed. "I'm so glad she didn't notice you."

As she was biting into a filled Santa donut, Desirae looked at their work tables and said, "I just thought of something. How are we going to get all the finished toys out of here without being seen?"

"That's actually two different problems. First, we have to find a way to easily transport the toys up the winding staircase. Second, we have to find a way to transport them out of the school so we can deliver them secretly to the different toy drives around the city," said Evan. "I have to admit I didn't think this through yet. We might have to resort to the pulley system we used before."

"Oh no! That day we used your gizmo wasn't fun. One thing for sure is that I better start wrapping these presents. We should have some type of coding system too so that we know what's in the package once we wrap it," said Desirae. "We want to drop off different toys at each location."

"Do we have gift wrap?" asked Shiloh.

"Yes!" exclaimed Evan. He walked over to a tall, grey, metal cabinet. Then, he opened both doors at the same time. Long rolls of colorful wrapping paper fell out. Above on a shelf were the other needed supplies: scotch tape, ribbons, and bows.

"Well, I guess I can get started!" exclaimed Roxy. "I love wrapping gifts."

"I like your idea of a coding system," said Evan. "How about if we use mirror writing just like Leonardo da Vinci."

"I understand it in theory," said Desirae. "I would write it so that if the image was reflected in a mirror it would read like regular writing. I could probably do it, but it's going to take me some time to master it."

"I can do it," said Evan. "I can even write it like Leonardo."

"Is there anything you can't do, Evan?" Roxy asked as she looked at him admiringly. Shiloh looked uncomfortable.

Evan blushed. Then, he took a sheet of paper and wrote:

toy boat
cloth ragdoll
toy train
wind up cat

He followed it up with mirror writing in penmanship that looked like da Vinci's.

$$\text{Toad pot}$$

$$\text{Mobzor Holo}$$

$$\text{riort pot}$$

$$\text{Tao qu briw}$$

"Remind me to come to you if I ever need a copy of the Mona Lisa," said Desirae as she gazed at Evan's mirror writing. "Okay, Me and Roxy will wrap and you write. No one will be able to tell what's in the presents but us. Secret Santa rules! Shiloh, do you mind putting on the tags? Then, we can have an assembly line going."

"Sounds like a plan to me. I can't wrap gifts and I can't do the mirror writing either, so it's the perfect job for me," said Shiloh. "Besides I really like the idea of Santa in a detective suit!"

"Okay," said Evan. "It's getting late. Can you guys come back tomorrow? In the meantime, I'll think about how we're going to get these upstairs, out of Cornerstone, and distributed to our delivery locations without being unmasked!"

"I can come back tomorrow after I get my chores done," said Desirae. "Around noon, would that be okay?"

"That's what I was going to suggest," said Evan. "What about you two, Shiloh and Roxy?"

"I think I can do it. I'll text you guys if I can't," Roxy said.

"Let me see what my parents say," Shiloh replied. "If I told them what we were doing, I'm sure they would say it was okay."

"Absolutely not!" exclaimed Evan. "We have to remain completely secret otherwise we'll violate the mission of Secret Santa. We're Secret Santa's Secret Elves."

"I'll text you tomorrow morning to let you know," said Shiloh. "Meanwhile, I'll take another donut for the road. I forgot how much energy it takes me to bike here. How are you guys getting home?"

"I'm going to call my brother for a ride home," said Roxy.

"I'm going to walk," said Desirae.

"I'm going to walk Desirae home and then I'm going to text my mom. She said she'd be glad to pick me up," said Evan. "She just thinks I had a science activity at school, which technically this is."

"Does she know about the lab?" asked Shiloh.

"No, I'd like to tell her...someday," said Evan.

Shiloh wasn't looking forward to the cold ride back home on his bike. He was about to ask Evan if they could both walk Desirae home and then go back in Evan's mom's car. After all, he lived right next door to Evan and Evan's mom had transported him back and forth to school many times.

But before he could say anything, Evan glared at him. That's when he realized that Evan wanted some alone time with Desirae without him around. "Okay, guys, I'm going to head out. Any particular donut you don't want me to take?" asked Shiloh.

"I'd like the last strawberry filled one," said Roxy.

Shiloh waved goodbye and munched on the chocolate donut with white icing that he'd picked from the box. He climbed up the metal staircase and went out the "laff Only" door. When he got outside, he realized that it was going to be far too cold to bike home. Snow was coming down pretty heavily.

He thought about asking Roxy for a ride but decided not to because he didn't know if she lived anywhere close to him.

Shiloh took out his phone and texted his dad.

> Hey, Dad. Could you
> or Mom come pick me
> up? The snow is
> really coming down.

Even with his heavy coat on, Shiloh was shivering. His dad texted back.

Your mom said she
would. She said she
can be there in 15
minutes. OK?

Shiloh's fingers were so cold that he
was having trouble texting.

Thanks, Dad. Tell
Mom I'm on the west
side right near the
flagpole.

In a minute, his dad texted back:

See you soon!

Just as she had promised, his mom
showed up in fifteen minutes, but it
seemed much longer to Shiloh since
it was so cold out. She quickly
opened the car door for him to hop
in. "You must be freezing!" she said.

"I tried to get here as soon as I could."

"Thanks, Mom. I really appreciate that you dropped everything to come and get me," said Shiloh. His teeth were still chattering.

"Of course! I'm glad you texted instead of trying to brave this weather," said his mom.

"How did the snow shoveling go today?" Shiloh asked.

"It was actually kind of fun. Your dad threw a snowball at me and I threw one back," she said. "He missed. I didn't." She laughed and flexed her arm. "Did you and Evan have fun with your science project?"

"Yeah," said Shiloh. "Evan and I always have fun when we get together. Roxy was there too." Shiloh wanted to tell his mom about the Secret Santa project, but he decided he would wait.

"Roxy was there? That's nice," she said with a wink.

"Mom!" Shiloh looked embarrassed. "Please don't wink. That is so cringe."

"Ok, ok. Tomorrow night Evan's mom and I have decided that our two families should have a little holiday get together. Since we're right next door, we're always roaming around in each other's houses during the holiday, but we've never had an official Christmas party. We were thinking of exchanging gifts too, you know, like Secret Santa," said his mom. "Of course, we'll have to pick names out of a jar and then have another get-together before Christmas so we can exchange our gifts. So, we don't spend too much, each gift has to be under $25."

Shiloh smiled to himself. "Do you think Evan's mom has mentioned the party and the gift exchange to him?"

"No, I don't think so, honey. It was actually my idea to extend our Secret Santa tradition to include them too. The more we chatted about it, the more it seemed like it would be fun," said Shiloh's mom.

"I'm not sure I have $25 in my allowance fund right now," said Shiloh.

"Oh, don't worry about that. The parents will give you guys the money to spend as long as you promise to get as close to $25 as possible and not spend it on yourself instead!" she said. "Maybe you can help me think of what snacks I can serve tomorrow night."

"Okay," said Shiloh. He was so filled up with donuts that he couldn't think about more food without his stomach feeling queasy.

"By the way, what were you eating today?" his mom asked. "Your mouth has chocolate on it."

"Sorry," said Shiloh. "Desirae brought us some donuts."

"Better clean up before your dad sees you!" exclaimed his mom with a twinkle in her eye. "Otherwise we'll get the anti-sugar speech."

Chapter 5

The Official Christmas Party

When they got home, Shiloh went up to his room for a while. He was surprised at how tired his hands were from all the sanding and painting he'd done on the toys for their Secret Santa project. He was trying to figure out what he could say to his parents so he could escape to the secret lab the next day. Since they were going to have Evan's family over it didn't make sense that he would want to spend the afternoon with Evan too. Both families getting together for a party seemed like a great idea and it made Shiloh wonder why none of them had thought about it before.

I can't wait to be a grown up and not have to always explain where you're going and who you're going to be with, Shiloh thought to himself. Shadow always seemed to be able to sense when Shiloh had something on his mind. He ran into Shiloh's

68

room and jumped up on the bed. He licked Shiloh's hand and looked into his face as if to ask, *What's wrong?*

Shiloh rubbed the fur on Shadow's back. Shadow closed his eyes and sprawled out on the bed as if he were getting a massage at a spa. It made Shiloh smile to see Shadow so relaxed. After they had spent a few minutes and had both almost started to doze off, Shiloh suddenly stretched and got up. He had to make a decision. He had to approach his dad or his mom to ask about tomorrow. His parents usually presented a united front, but they also didn't like to change their minds if one of them had already said yes to something. He decided he would try talking to his mom first.

He went downstairs to the kitchen. His mom was starting to bang pots around in preparation for dinner. During the holidays, she always fixed lots of stews, soups, and chili. There was always so much to do that she would often prepare them and put them in the crockpot to slow cook. The kitchen was warm and the aroma smelled amazing, but Shiloh couldn't identify exactly what she was making yet.

"Whatcha making, Mom?" Shiloh asked as he poked about. Shadow had followed him down to the kitchen and was sniffing the air.

"Hi, honey. I thought you and Shadow were taking a nap," said his mom. "We're going to have chili, cornbread, and a salad for dinner tonight." She was chopping some onions which were making tears streak down her face.

"Yum! Chili sounds great. The cold weather always makes me hungry for chili. Shadow and I weren't sleeping. We were just relaxing. My hands were tired from working on Evan's project with him," Shiloh said. "I can chop the rest of those for you if you want. They don't make my eyes burn too much."

"Would you? That would be great," said his mom. "I wonder why your eyes don't burn and mine always do. Are you sure you don't mind since you said your hands were tired?" Shiloh didn't often offer to help in the kitchen so she suspected that he was going to ask for a favor. He must think she was born yesterday. Her children were so predictable.

"Nah, I'm not that tired!" Shiloh said. He washed his hands at the kitchen sink and then took over the onion chopping.

His mom started to put ingredients into the crockpot. "What do you think...should I make gumbo or stew for the party tomorrow night?" she asked as she glanced sideways at Shiloh.

"Wow! You're going to make dinner for everybody? I thought we were just going to have mini corn dogs or pizza," said Shiloh. He was trying to sway his mom into making his favorite food.

"No, I changed my mind. I thought it would be lovely if we all sat down together. That reminds me I've got to ask your dad to help me put the extender in the table," his mom said as she scribbled a note to herself.

"I vote for gumbo. We haven't had that in a long time," said Shiloh.

"That's what I was thinking too. It's so colorful and fun. I can serve it with some rice in our red Christmas bowls," she said.

Shiloh smiled and then for a few minutes he and his mom just worked on the chili. There were quite a few onions to chop and as he finished, she threw them into the crockpot. Then, she started looking through her spice cabinet for the chili powder.

"Mom, I've got a favor to ask," said Shiloh.

Here it is. His mom had been waiting for a while. It was nice to have hi help cook but she was getting impatient waiting for the favor.

"What is it?"

"Is it okay with you if I go back to Cornerstone tomorrow and help Evan with his project?" Shiloh asked. "He really needs my help to finish it."

"I'm really surprised that the school building is open on a Sunday," said Shiloh's mom.

"Yeah, there's a lot going on since school is going to be closed for Christmas next week," said Shiloh.

"Well, I was hoping we could all decorate the tree tomorrow before Evan's family comes over," she said, "but if it's that important, it's okay with me."

"Thanks, Mom," said Shiloh as he chopped up the last piece of onion. "Is there anything else you need, Mom?"

"No, I'm good," said his mom. "We should be ready to eat in about 40 minutes."

Shiloh had his phone in his pocket and he could feel it go off. It was Evan.

```
Are you coming
tomorrow?
```

Shiloh texted back.

```
My mom said yes.
I'll be there, noon
sharp.
```

In just a few seconds, Evan texted back.

```
AWESOME!!!!!
```

Shiloh sent another text.

> Did you know our
> moms decided that?
> our families should
> exchange gifts
> as Secret Santa?
> We're picking names
> tomorrow after
> dinner.

There was no response from Evan
for a few minutes. Shiloh could
almost hear the gears in Evan's brain
turning from his house next door.

> What??? Oh no!!! Do
> you think they
> figured out?
> what we're doing?

Shiloh replied.

> Nope. I think it's
> a coincidence. I
> haven't said
> anything. It was my
> mom's idea and I
> know she doesn't
> know.

As Shadow followed him, Shiloh went back upstairs. He searched on the internet for a map that would show all the donation centers for children's toys. Surprisingly, he found a simple map that showed exactly what he was looking for. The locations were clearly marked and there were also schedules showing when the locations were open and how late Christmas gifts could be dropped off to make sure they were delivered in time.

According to the map, they only had a few more days to get the Secret Santa gifts there. Santa's elves had to get moving! Shiloh was wondering how many additional days they would need to finish their goal of 100 toys.

Shiloh downloaded the map and printed it. He didn't use the printer in his room all that often and it was almost out of color ink. The map printed out in strange color tones, but all the locations and information could be seen. He printed out enough copies for the four "elves" to each have two maps.

"Time for dinner!" his mom called out from the kitchen. The smells of the delicious chili were floating throughout the house.

***

The next day, Shiloh was just about to go into the garage to get his bike when his mom stopped him.

"Do you need a lift?" she asked.

"That would be great, Mom," Shiloh said. He knew it was a risk having her come to Cornerstone, but it was still so cold out that riding his bike wasn't an option.

"Let's take your bike just in case it warms up a bit and you have to bike back. The Christmas party starts at 6:00, but if you want a lift please call me by 4:00," she said. Shiloh nodded, grabbed his bike, and loaded it in the back of his dad's car.

After they got out of the garage and started down the road, his mom asked, "What exactly are you and Evan working on? I hope it's nothing dangerous."

"No, it's not dangerous, but I can't really talk about it because...because we're supposed to keep it under wraps for now. But trust me, you'll be really surprised and you'll love it," Shiloh said. He didn't want to hide it from his mom, but he knew that Evan would be really upset if he told her before they accomplished their plan.

"Ok, I trust you. Here we are," said his mom. "I'll wait here just in case it's locked and you can't get in."

"That's okay. Evan's inside. He just texted me so he can let me in," said Shiloh.

"Okay. Have a good time," said his mom. She was very curious about what they were planning but she knew that Evan was a smart kid with a good heart so she decided to be patient and wait for them to tell her what was going on.

As soon as Shiloh got into Santa's Secret Lab, he wondered how early Evan and Desirae arrived. There were piles of toys everywhere and an entire stack that were wrapped and waiting to be tagged with the special Secret Santa tags.

"Wow! What's happening? You guys have gotten so much done," said Shiloh.

"We stayed a couple more hours after you left last night and we got started about an hour ago today," said Evan.

Desirae smiled. "It's so much fun. I just wish we could see the children's faces when they open the toys."

Just then Roxy also came down. Her face was flushed and she was breathing hard.

"How did you get in and why are you so out of breath?" Evan asked, looking alarmed.

"I saw you let in Shiloh and I ran to catch the door. I managed to put my foot in the wedge just before it shut," she said.

Evan had Christmas music playing and the lights had been dimmed, but they were still flickering on and off in time to the music.

"What do you want us to do first?" asked Shiloh.

"Well, we've sort of lost count. It would be good to have an idea of how much we've finished and how many more we need to do to get to 100," Evan said.

"Yeah, and as you can see, we need for the tags to be put on," said Desirae.

"Oh! I almost forgot. I have something that might be helpful," said Shiloh as he pulled the copies of the map out of his backpack.

Evan took a quick glance at the map and said, "It's perfect! Where did you find this?"

"I googled it," said Shiloh. "I just did a quick search online and there it was."

"There's only one problem. We can't walk or bike the gifts to the locations. They're too far away," said Evan.

"We could use some flying reindeer," said Roxy as she laughed.

"Or some Secret Santa drones," said Shiloh.

"That's it! Shiloh, you're a genius!" said Evan.

"What do you mean?" asked Shiloh. He was trying to read one of Evan's mirrored labels on one of the packages, but he couldn't make it out.

Evan walked up to another grey metal cabinet along the opposite wall from the wrapping paper cabinet. Roxy, Desirae and Shiloh stopped what they were doing and followed him.

Evan opened up the cabinet. Inside were circular white pieces and pieces that looked like small flying propellers.

"What are these?" asked Desirae. "They look like drones that snap together."

"That's exactly what they are!" exclaimed Evan proudly. "I went on YouTube and found videos that helped me improve on their design."

Chapter 6

Secret Santa's Delivery System

"This is amazing, Evan!" said Shiloh. "When did you do this?"

"I've been working on it for a while," said Evan, "but when I first snapped the pieces together the propellers wouldn't fire in sync so they wouldn't fly properly. I think I have the bugs worked out now, but we should probably do a test run. Each drone by itself can carry 5 pounds, so if you need to lift 20 pounds then 4 of them have to be snapped together in a square."

"Maybe we should get a few of the non-breakable toys and test it," said Desirae.

"That's probably a good idea." said Evan. "I don't know why I didn't think of using this as a delivery system before. I must have had brain fog."

"This is so cool. I want to try flying one," said Shiloh.

"Okay," said Roxy. "Let's try the 5-pound version first." She quickly assembled a mini-version of Santa's red velvet toy bag and put two of the toys in it.

Evan quickly snapped together the pieces for one drone. There was a safety hook at the bottom to carry the mini-bag.

Then, he handed the controls to Shiloh and quickly showed him how to work it. "Okay, here we go," said Shiloh. The drone took off and headed toward the model train and Christmas village. At first, it seemed to be spinning around wildly and it took some practice for Shiloh to get it under control so it was smooth.

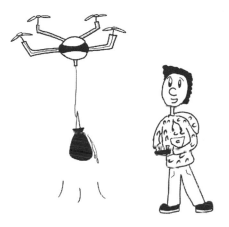

Within a few minutes, Shiloh had the drone flying in and out and over gracefully. It was exciting to see it flying around the Christmas decorations, Desirae and Roxy were clapping their hands with glee in time to the music and Evan looked like a proud father whose children had just done something amazing.

After Shiloh had flown the drone around for a full five minutes, he carefully landed it on Desirae's worktable almost as if it were a plane on a runway.

"Wow! That was so much fun!" exclaimed Shiloh. "What's next?"

"You did a great job, Shiloh. You handled the controls much better than I do. I think you should be our official pilot," said Evan. "Next we should test a heavier payload. I think we should try 20 pounds." Evan quickly snapped together four of the circular drones into a square pattern.

Desirae prepared a bag that had six toys. She weighed it at 19 pounds. "This is close enough," she said.

As soon as everything was prepared, Shiloh began operating the controls. The heavier drone took off more slowly than the first one had, but that actually made it easier for Shiloh to fly it. He soon had it flying over the rooftops of the Christmas village and around and under the Christmas lights. After a few minutes of testing, he landed it safely on Desirae's worktable.

"I think we're ready. There's only one problem. How are we going to do this without anyone from Cornerstone seeing us?" Evan asked as he gazed out over the pile of wrapped toys.

But, before they could solve that problem, Shiloh said, "What about the different locations? How will I know how to steer the drone to them?"

"That part isn't as hard as you think. I have an app that shows exactly where they are flying on the map so you can adjust as it's flying. It has a small camera too. When you get closer to the actual destination, you can turn on the camera to drop the mini-Secret Santa bag at the entrance," said Evan.

"Okay. We need to wrap this up. Let's count everything, make sure it's all wrapped and tagged and ready for delivery. We'll need to mark the weight of each bag too," said Roxy. "It's already one o-clock and you guys said you had to leave at four. We still have a lot to do."

The four friends spent the rest of the afternoon organizing the toys for their Secret Santa project. They had already completed 90 toys so they only had a few more to finish. By 3:45, everything was wrapped up.

"I've got it!" said Evan. "We've got to fly the drones early in the morning before classes start tomorrow."

"How early?" asked Shiloh.

"I think we should meet here at 5:00 am," said Evan. "We're going to have to move lightning fast in order to finish everything."

"What? 5:00 am?" asked Shiloh.

"But, Evan, even if we could get here that early, the locations won't be open to receive the toys," said Desirae.

"I've thought about that," said Evan. "We'll just have to deliver the toy bags as close to the front door as possible. Then when the managers of the toy drives arrive there in the morning, they'll take them indoors."

"But, someone could steal the toys," said Desirae.

"That's true, but if they do, they'll be on camera and caught red-handed!" exclaimed Evan.

"I have no idea how I'm going to escape from home and come to Cornerstone that early. Can you text me to wake me up?" asked Shiloh.

"Sure, I'll text all of you. Do you think your mom would mind giving all four of us a lift back today?" asked Evan.

"I'm sure she'd be fine with that. Desirae, Roxy, have you guys ever met my mom?" asked Shiloh.

"Yes, we met when we were doing the play performances at the Leroux Theater a couple of months ago," said Desirae.

"I forgot all about that. I'll text her right now," said Shiloh.

***

Later that evening, Shiloh's mom was taking care of the last-minute preparations for dinner. The tree had already been trimmed and she had, with some help from Shasha and Shiloh's dad, done a wonderful job decorating the house. Even though all the decorations were artificial, there were pine candles so the house smelled like Christmas too. There was a light snow falling and everything looked picture perfect. Shasha had already set up the Secret Santa jar. Everybody's names had been put on slips of paper. After dinner, each person was supposed to pick a name. Of course, if they picked their own name, they would have to put it back in the glass jar and mix everything up again.

It was soon six o'clock and the doorbell rang out a Christmas tune as Evan's family arrived. Will was dressed as an elf, but everyone else wore their casual clothes as Shiloh's mom had let them know in advance that it would be a "no-fuss" party.

Dinner wasn't quite ready so everyone sat in the living room. Shadow took an immediate liking to Will and Will took off his red and white elf hat and stuck it on Shadow's head, which made everyone laugh.

The parents made small talk as Evan and Shiloh spoke in hushed tones about their project. They were sitting at a table where Shiloh's mom had set up a huge 2,000-piece puzzle. The puzzle was a chaotic Christmas scene with a comical Santa, Mrs. Claus, and lots of funny-looking elves making toys. Once again, she seemed to have a sixth sense about what was going on with Shiloh and Evan. There were only a few pieces put together and as the two of them were talking Shasha wandered over.

She looked at the big pile of pieces and the cover art and quickly put together one side of the puzzle. Shiloh looked at her and asked, "How'd you do that so fast?"

"I always look for the straight-edged pieces first and try to put together the entire perimeter," she said smugly. "By the way, you too seem like you're planning a bank robbery with all the whispering you're doing."

"If we were planning something, it would be the opposite of a robbery," said Evan.

Shasha didn't understand what Evan was getting at, but by now she had discovered that Shiloh's best friend wasn't easy to figure out so she had given up trying. She just smiled and put together a few more puzzle pieces before wandering off to play with Will and Shadow.

Shiloh's mom disappeared into the kitchen and came back with a plate of appetizers. She had promised Shiloh that she would fix mini corn dogs since those were his favorites along with her famous stuffed mushrooms. Shiloh resisted the urge to take all of them for himself.

Everyone was chatting and having a great time. Suddenly, a bell went off and for a minute no one realized it was the kitchen timer. "Gumbo's ready!" said Shiloh's mom.

They all went into the dining room. Evan's mom had brought over a special chair for Will so that he could sit at the adult table. The smell of the gumbo had filled the dining room and everyone couldn't wait to eat. Shiloh's mom led grace and then they dug in. The gumbo was hearty and flavorful and coupled with the white rice in their Christmas bowls gave the table a special holiday feeling.

Shiloh was thinking about how grateful he was that even though his parents were quite different from Evan's they all seemed to get along. If they all knew what he and Evan and Desirae had been doing they would have been proud.

After dinner, everyone sat in the living room until Shiloh's mom and dad cleared off the table. When they were finished they joined everyone.

"Okay," said Shasha. "It's time to pick the names for Secret Santa. Evan's mom will help Will choose and buy his gift, which means that Will can't pick his own name or his mom's."

"There are a few other rules as well," said Shiloh's mom. "The gift you select must cost less than $25 and it must be tiny and fit in someone's pocket. All non-adults will be given the budget to spend courtesy of their parents. On the outside of your wrapped gift you should put the name of the person who's going to receive the gift and make sure you list that it's from Secret Santa. Don't put your own name!"

"I'm glad you're funding us, but it's still going to be tough," said Shiloh. "Why does it have to be so small?"

"Because your mom and I have decided that we'll all exchange our gifts at the Christmas House Tour this coming week so we can't be

carrying large items around," said
Evan's mom.

"I'm excited! I always wanted to go
on the house tour!" exclaimed
Shasha. "Everyone dresses so fancy.
It's very exciting. They sometimes
have carolers or readings."

"That sounds like fun," said Evan's
dad.

The jar went around the room twice
before everyone had picked a name
that wasn't their own.

Some of them knew what to buy,
but others had no idea. They only
had five days to buy their gifts, wrap
them, and bring them along the
night of the tour.

Chapter 7

Secret Santas Revealed

When Shiloh woke up the next morning, he had no idea what time it was. The room was dark and Shadow was curled up on top of the blanket over Shiloh's feet. Then, Shiloh realized that his phone must have been beeping for some time. He had put it right by his pillow so that he could hear Evan's wake-up text. He looked at the alarm clock. It was 15 minutes to 4 am. He had taken a shower the night before after their Christmas party was over. His parents had found that suspicious since he usually showered in the morning, but they didn't say anything to him.

Evan had sent this message.

```
Wake up, sleepy
Santa's elf!
It's time for the
toys to fly off the
shelf!
```

> Get here by 5 and
> don't be late,
> It's our Secret
> Santa shipping
> date.

Shiloh rolled his eyes. Sometimes he was so cringe. He wondered how in the world Evan could be awake and able to rhyme in the middle of the night. He wandered into the bathroom and threw some cold water on his face. He dressed in his warmest clothes. Shadow woke up and Shiloh tried to keep him quiet. He really needed to escape before anyone found out what he was doing.

He was ready to head out in 15 minutes, but getting downstairs without making a sound wasn't going to be easy. As Shiloh headed down the stairs, he winced at every creak. He had never noticed that before. Usually there was so much noise in the house that such a tiny noise wouldn't be noticeable, but it was so quiet in the middle of the night that the sound seemed really loud. He was cringing. What was he going to do if Shasha or his parents woke up?

He was keeping his fingers crossed that no one woke up. When he got down to the kitchen, he wrote a quick note—*had to leave for school early, see you tonight!*
He figured that by the time anyone saw it, they wouldn't know what time he had left.

Right before he opened the door, he said to Shadow. "Now go upstairs, boy. I've got something to do and you can't come along. I'm sorry." Shadow whined a little, but then he headed back up the stairs. It was bone-chillingly cold outdoors. *Why did I agree to do this?* Shiloh thought to himself.

As soon as he parked his bike at Cornerstone, he ran up to the front door, but it was locked. He texted Evan and Evan came running up to the front to let him in.

"How did you get in?" Shiloh asked.

"I have my ways," said Evan. "Let's just say that the school's security system isn't that difficult to get around. That's why we have to keep everything locked up so no one will know we were here."

Evan had already set up a basket gizmo system so they could get the toys out of the school. Desirae and Roxy arrived a few minutes later and Evan had to run to the front again to let them in.

As soon as they were all in the Secret Lab, Evan made an announcement. "Okay, this is what we're doing. First, we're going to get all the toys and take them from the lab to the hallway outside the "Iaff Only" door. Then, we're going to bring them outside in the plastic buckets that I've already stuck out in the hallway. I've set the drones up outdoors already. The maps and the apps are ready to go so as long as our pilot is awake enough to fly the drones, we're all set."

Shiloh was yawning as he said that. "I'm awake! What time did you get here?" asked Shiloh.

"At 2 am," said Evan. "Santa's elves don't get any rest during the holiday."

"How are we going to get the drones back here before class starts?" Shiloh asked.

"We're not," said Evan. "I've positioned my backyard as the drop-off zone. So after the toys have been delivered, you'll fly the drones back to my house. Don't worry everything is pre-programmed. Just keep the drone on the map and going to the correct location and everything will be fine. We won't try to do all the trips at once. We've got a little over two hours before some of the teachers show up."

"We better get moving," said Roxy.

It only took the four of them about half an hour to get the toys upstairs with Evan's system. The baskets that Evan had attached to go up and down on the pulleys were able to hold 20 wrapped gifts so it only took five trips.

Once they had everything in the hallway, they lugged things outdoors rapidly. Within minutes they had the first drone ready to take off. They had decided to limit the trips to 10 toys at each location. Most of the toys were lightweight so a pair of two drones snapped together was perfect for a group of ten.

Shiloh took the controls. They were ready to send the first drone out. It was packed with a red velvet bag containing the first 10 toys. "Okay," said Shiloh. "I'm ready!" As the white drone took off into the falling snow with its red velvet bag of Christmas toys, the three friends shared a special moment. Flying off into the distance, it seemed more like a Christmas angel bearing gifts than a mechanical object.

"This is so cool," said Desirae. "I'm never going to forget this Christmas."

"I feel the same way," said Evan as he looked at her. He tried to burn everything into his memory so he could tell his and Desirae's children someday.

"I'll feel better once all the toys are delivered. I just hope we wrap up before 7 am," said Roxy.

They finished everything 10 minutes before the first teachers arrived at the school.

As Shiloh was sending the last drone out, Evan, Desirae, and Roxy went back indoors to turn off the lights to the secret lab.

"Are we going to come back here during the holiday?" asked Desirae.

"We might," said Evan. "Merry Christmas, Desirae."

"Merry Christmas, Evan," she said. "I've had such a good time these last few weeks."

"Me too," said Evan.

Desirae smiled and Evan could see her eyes shining even though the room was almost dark. Then, she hugged him.

Evan felt so much happiness on the inside he thought he would burst. He couldn't say anything. He could feel his cheeks turning as red as Christmas ornaments.

Desirae then turned to Shiloh and Roxy and hugged them too. "I'm so happy we could all do this together!"

The four friends gathered in the hallway before heading out to homeroom.

Shiloh noticed that Evan's cheeks were red, but he didn't say anything. "Bye, Evan!" he said. "Catch you later."

"Thanks, Shiloh. You're a great pilot!" said Evan. He watched Shiloh, Desirae, and Roxy walk away. Even though Ms. Sufferin was their homeroom teacher, he wished he was going with them. It was going to be difficult to be away from Desirae during school break.

It was 10 minutes before class was supposed to start as Shiloh and Desirae slid into their respective seats. Ms. Sufferin was out in the hallway talking to Mr. Thomas. As soon as Shiloh sat down he realized how tired he was. He stretched his legs out for a second. He wedged his head on one of his shoulders and then started to doze off.
He hadn't even taken his jacket off.

The bell rang, but he didn't wake up. Ms. Sufferin began to walk toward him with her pointer. Her heels were making squeaky sounds on the floor, but he still didn't wake up. Desirae couldn't see Shiloh's face from the back of the class, but she could see Ms. Sufferin descending upon him like a giant raven. *Oh no!* she thought to herself, *poor Shiloh!*

Ms. Sufferin slammed her pointer down on Shiloh's desk. Shiloh opened one eye.

"I'm sorry. Did I wake you?" She asked sarcastically. "I was pleased to see that for once you were here on time, but now you've decided that you don't need to be awake. I suppose the excitement of the season has caught up with you. Have you been partying away after class?"

"Yes, I mean no, Ms. Sufferin," Shiloh mumbled. He was still half asleep and was having a vision of her being carried away by a giant drone. It was a happy thought. There were muffled giggles from the rest of the class.

"Please sit up straight and get those enormous clodhoppers out of the aisle!" she said as she slammed the pointer on the outer side of his right boot.

Shiloh pulled his legs in. He was getting a little too tall for the middle grade desks and his knees touched the bottom of the desktop. *I can't believe I fell asleep,* Shiloh thought to himself.

He tried to be especially attentive for the rest of homeroom, but Ms. Sufferin was in a bad mood until she noticed that someone had left a teeny tiny gift on her desk. Shiloh noticed that the gift had one of Desirae's Secret Santa tags on it. The tag was almost as large as the gift. Maybe Mr. Thomas had brought the gift, but how would he have gotten one of Desirae's tags?

After homeroom was over, he caught Desirae in the hall and asked her about it. "Desirae, did you put that gift on Ms. Sufferin's desk?"

"Yes, I usually buy something tiny for each of my teachers, but I don't want them to know that it's from me," said Desirae. "I don't want to be called a teacher's pet so I choose the secret route."

"What did you get for her?" Shiloh asked. He couldn't imagine buying a gift that would suit Ms. Sufferin.

"Secret Santa doesn't divulge secrets," she said as she smiled.

***

School was out for the holiday break by midweek and Shiloh and Evan's families were busy shopping for their Secret Santa gifts.

Shiloh was excited that he had picked Will's name from the Secret Santa jar. He hadn't bought a Christmas present for a little kid before and he was trying to think about the kinds of toys he loved when he was Will's age.

Their parents had taken him and Shasha to the mall so they could shop. When they got there, his mom said, "Okay, everyone make a note of the time. It's 4:30 now, we'll meet back here at 6:30 and then we'll go out for burgers. How does that sound?"

"Fun!" said Shasha. Shasha had picked Evan's name from the Secret Santa jar. Even though Shiloh was endlessly talking about his friend, Shasha didn't really have any idea what to buy for him. Despite that, she was in a good mood, because being at the mall during the holidays was always fun.

Shiloh's dad had picked Shiloh's name and he had lots of ideas for Shiloh's gift but none of them were less than $25 or fit in a pocket. He was stumped. "I need help," he said to Shiloh's mom.

"Nope! Sorry, but you're on your own and don't tell me who you're buying for," she said. "As it is, I'm stumped too! I was hoping that I would get someone easy to buy for, but no such luck!" She had picked Evan's dad and he was the one person in Evan's family that she didn't know very well.

As they all split up, Shasha wandered into the bookstore. She knew that Evan was bookish so she thought it was a good bet that she could find something for him there. She was leafing through the pages of a book when she heard a familiar voice.

"Hey, Shasha! Merry Christmas!" said Shayna. "I was going to call you today."

"Merry Christmas!" said Shasha. She was thrilled to have run into her best friend and she gave her a big hug.

"My mom said I could invite you and a few of my other friends for a party a couple of days before New Year's," Shayna said. "I can't believe I ran into you."

"I'm sure my mom will say it's okay," said Shasha. *This holiday is shaping up to be fun,* Shasha thought to herself.

"Are you shopping for your family?" Shayna asked.

"No. I have a Secret Santa present to buy. Any ideas for a gift under $25 that fits into a pocket and is for a guy who is bookish," said Shasha.

"Sure," said Shayna. "You can buy a $25 gift card that he can use to buy whatever books he wants from this location or from the online store."

"That's perfect," said Shasha. "I'll buy it right now. Then, if you can, we can wander around until I have to meet my family in two hours."

"I only have one hour, but it would be fun if we can wander around together before I'm meeting my mom," said Shayna.

At 6:30 pm, the family met back up. Shiloh was carrying a huge bag.

"Shiloh, what's this? Whatever it is, it won't fit in a pocket," said his mom as she laughed.

"Yes, it will," said Shiloh. "I have a plan."

They all headed to their favorite burger place inside the mall. Shiloh's dad had picked up a newspaper. He was cruising through it while they were waiting for their food.

He opened the pages to the lifestyle section.

There was a big headline:

Angelic Drones Deliver 100 Secret Santa Gifts Throughout City

He began reading the article quietly. Shiloh saw the headline over his shoulder and gulped. After his dad had read the article, he looked up and said, "This story is amazing. Some anonymous person or group gave 100 toys as Secret Santa. No one knows who the gift giver is. There's some strange alien-looking script on the packages and no one can figure out what it says. The toys were delivered by circular white drones. The article compares the drones to angels with wings, but then it says the true angels were the gift givers. It's so nice to read a story like this during the holidays. It's good to know that some people still think of others before themselves. The Mayor wants to recognize the gift givers and are asking citizens to tell if they know the identity of those who gave so generously. They have pictures of some of the children who received the gifts. It's very touching."

Shiloh had just been served his burger and he took a big bite so that his dad wouldn't notice his reaction.

***

When they got home, Shiloh sent a text to Evan.

> Did you see the newspaper headline?

In a few minutes, Evan texted back:

> Yeah, it's so cool. My parents weren't around that day, so I was able to hide the drones before they got home and noticed them in the backyard. I loved being Secret Santa. We need to do it again next year.

Shiloh wrote back:

```
I loved the whole
thing, especially
flying the drones.
```

Later in the week, everyone had their Secret Santa gifts ready. It was time to meet up and go on the Christmas home tour.

They decided to start at the Leroux Mansion, the first home on the tour. The Leroux Mansion was about a block away from the Leroux Theater. The outside was covered with tiny flashing lights. The managers of the theater had their business offices there, but inside it was all decked out for the holidays with real trees and wreaths.

"Wow! This is just as beautiful as the theater," said Shasha when they stepped indoors.

"It's amazing," said Shiloh. "The original owners of the theater must have loved living here."

"Look! Here's some mistletoe," said Shiloh's dad as he put his arm around Shiloh's mom to give her a kiss. Shiloh's mom blushed.

In a few minutes, Evan and his family walked in.

"Evan, you look so handsome," said Shiloh's mom. "In fact, all of you look wonderful."

"Thank you, so do all of you!" said Evan as he bowed. He was wearing a dark green jacket with a red velvet bow tie. "Wow! This is incredible. I didn't think we'd see anything as grand as the theater."

"That's what we were saying," said Shasha, "but supposedly there are some homes on the tour that are even more spectacular."

As they all went from home to home, it was turning out to be a magical evening. Finally, they arrived at the last home on the list, the Gansley Mansion.

"I just can't wait to see what my clients have done with this home," said Shiloh's mom as she read the information from the brochure on their way there.

When they got there, they couldn't believe their eyes. Not only was the entire yard decked out with thousands of Christmas lights. It was also filled with a crowd of people. News trucks were in front and there were reporters with lights and microphones.

"What's going on??" Shiloh asked with complete wonder.

"I think we've been found out," Evan said in amazement.

When they got closer they saw that Roxy and Desirae and their families were on the lawn waiting for them.

"What? How?" Evan was flustered.

"We couldn't let this stay a secret any longer so we hatched a plan to tell the Mayor about our plan," Desirae said.

"But the whole point of a Secret Santa is to keep it a secret!" Evan exclaimed. He was so embarrassed by all the attention.

"Son, we knew it was you all along. We knew that you and your three friends were up to something and when we saw the article I knew it was you. There's no one in our town who could make those drones," Evan's dad said.

"We think it's wonderful that you four took time from your busy schedule and put in the work to spread Christmas cheer!" Shiloh's mom said to the group.

The Mayor made his way through the crowd and presented Shiloh, Evan, Roxy, and Desirae with a Good Samaritan award. He also encouraged others to be as creative and generous as these kids and reminded them that it was never too young to give back.

As Shiloh stood there, he thought of how happy he had felt to make the holiday more about others and not about himself. He looked at his friends and he decided that this was the best Christmas he ever had.

After the tour was over, they sat at one of the tables that had been set up in the Gansley Mansion. The owners came over to talk to them to tell them how happy they were to move to a community that was so interested in helping others.

Shiloh's family and Evan's family opened up their Secret Santa gifts. No one could figure out who their Secret Santa was. Shiloh's gift to Will was the most ingenious of all. He had drawn a map so that Will could find his Christmas gift over at Shiloh's house. Will thought the treasure map was his gift, but his gift was a toy robot waiting to be found in Shiloh's closet. Technically the map fit in Will's pocket so he didn't break the rules.

Acknowledgments

I want to thank my family again for their support. Your continual affirmation and encouragement is what keeps me going. I love you.

About the Author

Rita Onyx is a member of the Onyx Family who also include Mirthell, Shalom, Sinead, Shasha, and Shiloh. Together they have a successful social media and YouTube following with over 1 million subscribers and over 1 billion views across their channels. Check out Onyx Family, Onyx Kids, Onyx Life, Playonyx, and Cardionyx on Onyx Flix, YouTube, Prime Video, Facebook, Instagram, Twitter, and Amazon to find their new videos, books, and merchandise. You can also hear Rita Onyx along with the family on The Onyx Life Podcast.

Other Onyx Kids Books:

Getting to Know Onyx Kids

Onyx Kids Shiloh's School Dayz #1 –
The Sealed Locker

Onyx Kids Shiloh's School Dayz #2–
The Class Pet Fraud

Onyx Kids Shiloh's School Dayz #3 –
The Phantom of the School Play